Helping families of all species, one tadpole at a time.

Freeda the Frog™

and the Two Mommas Next Door

by Gold Mom's Choice Award® winner
Nadine Haruni

art by Tina Modugno

www.mascotbooks.com

Freeda the Frog™ and the Two Mommas Next Door

©2020 Nadine Haruni. All Rights Reserved. No part of this publication may be reproduced, stored in a retrieval system or transmitted in any form by any means electronic, mechanical, or photocopying, recording or otherwise without the permission of the author.

For more information, please contact:
Mascot Books
620 Herndon Parkway #320
Herndon, VA 20170
info@mascotbooks.com

Library of Congress Control Number: 2019919764

CPSIA Code: PRT0320A
ISBN: 978-1-64543-385-9

Printed in the United States

Foreword

Nadine Haruni has once again done an incredible job at allowing children to open up a discussion on a topic that may be initially difficult for them to interpret and grasp. This book is a testament to Nadine's dedication to writing about specific matters that are important for children of all ages to understand. In this brand-new addition to Nadine's Freeda the Frog series, children gain insight toward the acceptance and understanding of the different types of family structures that may exist. It relays that there isn't always just a mom and dad—there may also be two moms or two dads, or just one parent, and every family structure is beautiful in its own way. In the end, all that matters is love. This book is a great tool to utilize during a family discussion, as a therapeutic tool in counseling sessions, or even as a great read as part of a one-on-one conversation with a child. The characters in *Freeda the Frog and the Two Mommas Next Door* are highly relatable to children of all ages. We hope that you enjoy this wonderful new addition to this brilliant series.

– Huma Imtiaz, school psychologist in New York

"Gold Mom's Choice Award-winning children's author Nadine Haruni has helped children understand some difficult issues in the past through her children's books. In this new story, Freeda learns about families that look like mine—LGBT families. As one of the parents involved in a landmark New Jersey adoption case, I love this book and I'm happy to see a successful series like Freeda the Frog™ take on families like mine. Freeda truly helps families make sense of it all."

– Jon Holden Galluccio, author of *An American Family*, and successful plaintiff in a 1997 case affirming New Jersey as the first state in the nation to give gay couples adoption equality.

Personal Thoughts from the LGBTQ+ Community

"This touching story can etch into the minds of young people the worldview of inclusivity, for those that need to be accepted and for those that will learn to accept people's differences. Being a gay dad, this is especially important to me."

– Roberto M.

"As a gay dad, I am proud of the message this book delivers. It is an important and hopeful step in the way we all should approach our differences. This story is a useful tool to help small children understand the many ways to define a family."

– Dr. Joseph Sachs

"We loved Freeda the Frog and her message that not all families look the same. We wish we had her books to read to our kids when they were young."

– Chris Megale and Curt Wagner

"I didn't have models of families or sexuality that reflected my reality growing up. Everything was heteronormative representations of life: mom and dad living happy lives together, boys liking girls/girls liking boys. I couldn't relate to any of this. This story is multi-layered and for a kid who doesn't identify (completely or partially) with the heteronormative world, it's saying, 'It's ok to be different and people will still like you.' Truly beautiful and we need more of this!"

-Mike T.

"When I was growing up, I knew that families were often different from my own. I was a child of divorced parents, both of whom remarried, and had more kids. We were a patchwork of love. As I got older, I realized that I was different than my siblings because I was gay (still am). I didn't see the same future for myself as I saw for them. I didn't know any family that could be built for me. I had never seen one. I certainly had never read about one. A book that shows kids that there are different families is important. Showing a kid that has a happy future with a family is possible no matter who you love is monumental. I wish I had this type of story in my younger life, and I am grateful that it has arrived for the lives of so many."

-Jenn L.

"Although she's not a tadpole, my daughter, like Jessica, has two mommas. And, like Jessica, my daughter sometimes makes new friends who haven't previously encountered two-momma families. So, I am quite happy to add *Freeda the Frog and the Two Mommas Next Door* to her bookshelf because all kids, be they human or amphibian, benefit from seeing their families and realities reflected at least some of the time in the stories they read."

-Darcy G.

This book is dedicated to my mom, (the original) Freeda, husband Jon, and the special tadpoles in my life—Jake, Sam, Hannah, Adi, Yael, Max, Kayla, and Emma.

I also want to express my deep gratitude to all of our Freeda friends for their continued love and support by buying our books, going to our events, telling their friends, librarians, and teachers about us, and following our @freedathefrog pages on social media. Extra special thanks goes out to Morgan and Irosha, who have gone "beyond the call of duty" as Freeda friends, in supporting us.

I also want to thank all of our brave friends who have written us reviews and shared their sentiments with us about being a gay parent, or being a gay child who did not have books like this when they were younger.

Lastly, I wrote this book to dedicate it to all of the gay parents and families out there who have been waiting for a Freeda (or other) book to come along to help recognize how beautiful their family is, and remind everyone that "all you need is love."

Frannie, Frank, and Jack had a really great first year at their new school in Port Frogafly, and made a lot of nice friends. Aside from Kyle, Emerson, and Maxine, they also started hanging out with a new student named Jessica. Jessica had just moved from a different pond, and invited her new friends over after school one day.

When they swam into Jessica's lily pad home, Jessica gave her mom, Irene, a kiss hello, and said, "Hey Mom—I want you to meet my new tadpole squad from school!"

The group all said a big "Hi!" to Irene, who then made them an after-school snack of mosquito macaroons and dragonfly lollipops.

After eating their goodies, they decided to play a game of tag, followed by a competition to see who could catch the biggest fly. (It was a tie.)

When they went back inside, Jessica called out "Hi Momma!" to another woman standing beside Irene. Jessica turned back to her friends and said, "Hey guys, I want to introduce you to my Momma, Morgan."

The group said another big "Hi!" to Morgan, who greeted the group warmly before she left to run some errands. Morgan gave Irene a kiss goodbye on the way out. The tadpoles looked at each other, confused, while Jessica waved goodbye to Morgan.

"So...you have two moms?" asked Frannie.

"Yep," replied Jessica.

"Where's your dad?" Emerson asked.

"No dad! Just two mommas," Jessica answered.

Frank was confused. He had never met anyone with two moms before. He turned to Jessica and said, "Your parents are two moms??? That's so weird!"

Frannie nudged her brother and said, "*Frank!* That's so rude!"

Jessica said, "That's okay! Yes, I have two parents, just like you do, except I have two moms—just not a mom and a dad."

The tadpoles then went back to playing games, and soon the friends all left Jessica's lily pad to go to their own pads for dinner.

Freeda and Samson sat with the tadpoles at dinner and asked them about their day.

"It was great. After school, we hung out at our new friend Jessica's house, and met her two mommas," said Frank.

"That's so nice," Freeda remarked.

"Isn't that wrong?" Jack asked.

"No, it's not wrong at all, just different than our family," said Samson. "Parents are parents, and isn't it nice that not every family looks the same?"

Fly Milk
3.25

"That's true," said Frank, "but do two mommas love each other the same way a mommy and a daddy do?"

"You know how I love Samson," Freeda continued. "That's how Jessica's moms feel about each other. Love is love. No two families look alike."

"For example, some tadpoles have just one mommy, some have just one daddy, some have step-parents, some tadpoles have two parents that are a mommy and a daddy, and then some tadpoles may have two parents that are either two mommas or two daddies. There are lots of different types of parents and families out there."

"I think that's pretty cool," said Frank. "Do you think we could invite their family over for dinner on Friday night?" he asked.

"Sure," Freeda said. "I think that's a great idea."

With that, the three
tadpoles hopped up and
high fived one another, and
gave out a loud "Ribbit! Ribbit!"
which is frog-talk for "Woo-hoo!"

When the doorbell rang that Friday night, the tadpoles practically knocked each other over with excitement as they raced each other to grab the door first.

"Hi, come on in," Frannie said to Jessica and her two moms in the doorway.

Freeda and Samson then introduced themselves and said, "Welcome to our home."

"My, what a lovely lily pad you have," Morgan said. "Here—we made you this for dessert." And with that, Morgan handed Freeda a lovely blueberry fly pie. It was still warm and the scent filled the air.

"Oooh, this looks delicious! Thank you so much!" said Freeda. "Can I offer you some fly water?"

"That would be lovely," answered Irene.

"Let's all sit down to eat before the food gets cold. There's nothing worse than cold frogafly stew!" Samson said with a chuckle.

The two families sat down to eat, and they talked and talked (and talked) the night away—and a frogtastic time was had by all. When Freeda brought out the delicious fly pie for dessert, everyone started to dig in.

Suddenly, Frank looked up from his plate and said, "Irene, I have a question. At school, Zoey's dad always does the baking. Who does it in your family if there's no dad?"

Irene smiled and put her fork down. "Well, Morgan and I BOTH love to bake," she laughed. "That's how we got this delicious pie, after all!"

When the dishes were cleared, the family swam their guests to the door.

"Thanks so much for having us over," said Morgan. "We TOADally enjoyed ourselves, and look forward to doing this again soon."

"The pleasure was all ours," said Freeda. "We really enjoy meeting other nice families like yours and are so glad that the kids introduced us."

Jessica and her mommas waved goodbye as they hopped away back to their lily pad.

After they left, the tadpoles turned to their parents and Jack gave a grateful "Ribbit! Ribbit!" to his parents for having their new friends over.

"They love each other, just like our family does. You were right, Mom. All you need is love," said Frank.

"Yes, indeed," agreed Freeda.

Find all the words!

```
O S Z X L F N A V V T S C T P Q G O R E
Y R O T W I R V Z C H D P J O N R M P P
S P H M A O L O L M E D Q W R V W U Y P
K O Z O U D X Y G L M J P H T O W W G W
B R G M P M P E P S K V F O F S B D C Z
G T P M O P U O U A V U U M R F Q J B H
F F V A N J I F L K D O U O O I X G M D
U C R S C G C N K E S V B J G N B M V Y
N G J K B P X O G J S H I H A S D B Q Z
Q H G L R C O M V M G I F O F W A P I B
W F I M Q H G Y Q I I C F P L E A O N T
Z L D B O U G I E G Y H J P Y Z E S Z R
G B X O X M D N L E W Z Z I O A S P H C
C U W E F F M F J S Y O O N V G F Q E C
M Y G D B E F N J Z W M U G V A R W C U
Q V A Z V Y A Z Y E H K L Y X A N G V G
F D M O C B O S R V V M U F H I P L Y D
P J L O V E I S A L L Y O U N E E D S K
F U J J R Y N R Z Q H U W V A P R A B R
F N P A R E N T S F A M I L Y E I Z T C
```

Family	Ribbit	Love Is All You Need
Love	WooHoo	Tadpoles
Parents	Mommas	Frogs
Port Frogafly	Neighbors	Lily pad
Hopping	Fun	

Take Freeda with you on your family adventures! Color and cut out this Freeda pic, glue a popsicle stick to the back of it and *voila*—Flat Freeda! Then tag us in your pics at @Freedathefrog and message them to us on Facebook or Instagram for us to re-post.

Cut along the dotted lines for your very own bookmark!

Freeda the Frog™
and the Two Mommas Next Door
by *Gold Mom's Choice Award®* winner Nadine Haruni

art by *Tina Modugno*

Discussion Questions

1. Do you think all families look the same?

2. Do you have any friends who have two moms or two dads like Jessica does?

3. How would you make different types of families feel included?

4. Do you have any friends who ever felt left out because their family didn't look like everyone else's family?

Freeda and her family meet Jessica and her two mommas, Morgan and Irene. The tadpoles discover that families do not have to all look the same, and that all you need is love.

ISBN: 978-1-64543-385-9

Retail Price: $14.95 US

The *Freeda the Frog* series

Helping families of all species, one tadpole at a time.

www.freedathefrog.com

@freedathefrog

For additional information about the *Freeda the Frog*™ Children's Book series, Freeda the Frog™ products, Freeda the Frog™ news and events, and to order additional copies of any of the Freeda the Frog™ books, go to www.freedathefrog.com. Also be sure to follow Freeda the Frog™ on Instagram, Twitter, and Facebook @freedathefrog!

Check out the other books in the Freeda the Frog™ Children's Book series!

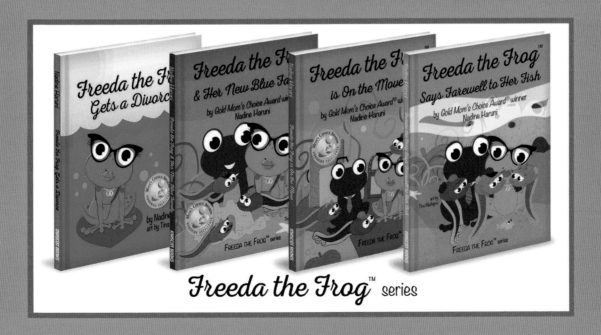

Freeda the Frog™ series

About the Author

Nadine Haruni is the author of the Gold Mom's Choice Award® winning *Freeda the Frog*™ Children's Book series, which focuses on different family situations and helping children cope with various life issues. Nadine is a member of the Society of Children's Book Writers and Illustrators and the Independent Book Publishers Association. Aside from writing, she teaches yoga and is a practicing attorney. Nadine is married with five children.

The first book of the series, *Freeda the Frog Gets a Divorce*, focuses on the difficult circumstances for children surrounding their parents' divorce. The second book, *Freeda the Frog and Her New Blue Family*, focuses on blended/step-families, as well as families of mixed race, religion, or ethnicity. The third book of the series, *Freeda the Frog is On the Move*, is geared toward helping kids cope with a move to a new school, town, or other major life change. The fourth book, *Freeda the Frog Says Farewell to Her Fish* focuses on dealing with the loss of a pet or loved one. Stay tuned for Nadine's future Freeda the Frog books, where Freeda and the tadpoles continue to help kids face more of life's challenges. Each book is a recipient of the Gold Mom's Choice Award® and have all received a Readers' Favorite five-star review.